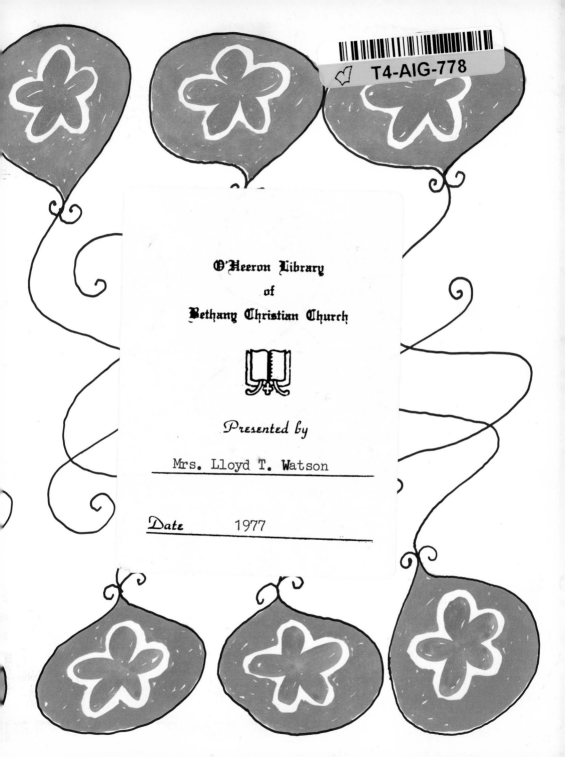

Mrs. Lloyd T Watson
Bethany Christian Church
Houston, Texas   77006

ILLUSTRATED BY
WILLIAM HUNTER

by
MARGARET O. SLICER

The Balloon Farm

ABINGDON PRESS Nashville ⚬ New York

THE BALLOON FARM is an expansion and
adaptation of "The Balloon Farm" by Margaret
O. Slicer, first published in *The Instructor* mag-
azine. Copyright assigned to Abingdon Press.

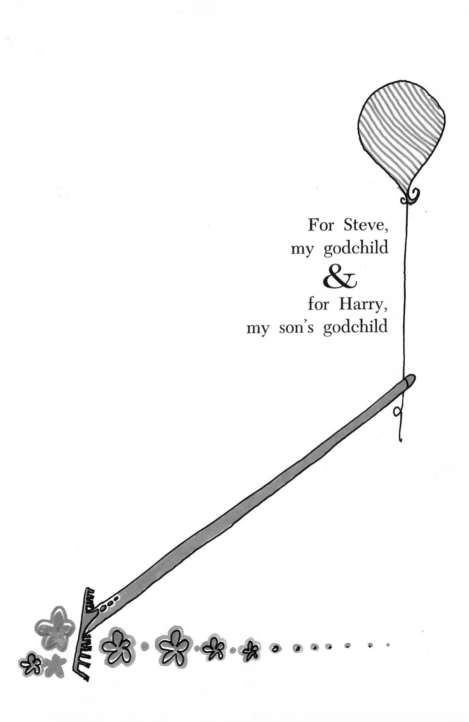

For Steve,
my godchild
&
for Harry,
my son's godchild

The small red carnival truck rattled along over the bumpy dirt road. Terry Malone sat up front with his father, who was driving, and with his mother, who was just holding on.

In the second seat in back was Wally Dressenfelder, the tall skinny barker who got people to come into the carnival tent at show time. Next to Wally was Tim Smoot, the short fat ticket-taker who took the people's money. Behind them in the truck was all the carnival

7

gear they could fit in—tent flaps, cook stoves, coils of
rope, popcorn machines, clown costumes, and bags of
gay-colored balloons.

Up ahead, also rattling down the road, were two more
carnival trucks. They were red, too, and they all three
had "Malone's Carnival Show" printed in big fancy black
letters on the side.

They were in Texas. Terry knew this because he had

asked Wally. Wally had been everywhere and knew a lot
of things.

"Yep," said Wally, leaning over the back of the front
seat to talk to Terry, "Yep, this is Texas, all right! We'd
be in the biggest state in the U. S. of A. except for Alaska.
But Texas is still mighty big!"

"How big?" asked Terry over his shoulder.

"Well," said Wally with a grin," it's almost as big as

9

the people around here think it is, and that's goin' some. Why, I hear there are some places in Texas so far away from other places in Texas that even the Texans don't know about them."

"You're fooling," said Terry.

"No, I'm not," said Wally. "Take Crazy County, for instance."

"Crazy County?" asked Terry. He unfolded a road map from the glove compartment. "I don't see it. Where is it?"

"The way I figure it," said Wally, "it's in the northeast, southwest corner of Texas and it's about five miles square."

"I still don't see it," said Terry, and then he thought a minute. "Did you say northeast, southwest corner? Why that's not—"

But Wally interrupted him. "You won't find it. Why should you? It's not important. No oil wells or cattle ranches or grapefruit orchards. All it has is—"

"Look!" cried Terry's mother, and she pointed out the window.

Terry looked. There stood an old signpost with a broken sign hanging from it. The worn letters said "Crazy County."

"We're there!" cried Terry. "Right this minute." He looked out across the brown flat land and said, "But I don't see anything. What did you say Crazy County had, Wally?"

"Dirt," said Wally. "Just miles and miles of brown dirt."

"But it looks like good dirt," said Mr. Malone, and

Terry heard his mother give a little sigh. She hated the carnival life of traveling all the time and wanted to settle down. Mr. Malone was always saying they would some-day, but he never could find a place he liked.

"Let's stop," said Terry.

"What for?" asked his father.

"I don't know, I just want to look," said Terry.

"We'll stop for gas at the next station," said Mr. Malone. "You can look around then. I want to ask directions anyhow. I think this map is out of date."

"It gives me a funny feeling, this place does," said Terry's mother. "I think something strange is going to happen."

But Terry couldn't see anything different about this flat brown country. It looked just like lots of other flat brown country he had seen in Texas.

Then they saw a small gas station just up the road, and after Terry's father had blown his horn to tell the other trucks to go on ahead, he pulled into the station and stopped. The other trucks would drive a few miles down the road looking for a place to spend the night and Terry's truck could catch up with them later.

They all got out to stretch their legs—Terry, his mother and father, and Wally and Tim. Mr. Malone checked the back of the truck to see if the tent flaps, cook stoves, coils of rope, popcorn machines, clown costumes, and bags of balloons were still all right.

Then they all went into the gas station to ask directions to the next town. Terry wanted a bottle of pop, but all they had was water and it wasn't cold. He felt hot and tired.

Mr. Malone asked the man in the gas station a lot of questions but the man didn't seem to know many of the answers. Finally Mr. Malone gave up.

"There must be some more road signs up ahead somewhere. We'll wait till we find them," he said. "Or maybe the others will have found out something when we catch up with them."

Terry's mother brushed back her hair with a tired hand. "I still get a funny feeling about this place," she said. But nobody paid any attention to her.

Then they went outside to get back in their truck— and stopped short. Another truck was standing by the gas pumps. The two trucks were exactly alike, but instead of "Malone's Carnival Show" the fancy letters on the second one said "Merryfield Farm," and as they went closer they could see that instead of tent flaps, cook stoves, coils of rope, popcorn machines, clown costumes, and bags of balloons inside, it was full of hoes and rakes, a wheelbarrow, bags of fertilizer, and a small plow. A farmer stood beside it, dressed in jeans and chewing on a straw. He looked like every picture of a farmer that Terry had ever seen. In fact, he did not look quite real, and Terry rubbed his eyes and looked again.

Then the farmer spoke. "How about a trade?" he said to Mr. Malone.

"A trade?"

"Sure," said the farmer without taking the straw out of his mouth. "Sometimes a fellow needs to try something new. Let's trade. Your truck for mine, your job for mine. I've always wanted to have a carnival of my own

ever since I used to run errands for the carnival folks when I was a kid. How big a show you got?"

"Big enough," said Mr. Malone, and Terry could see that he was thinking very hard. His mother stood by, twisting her hands together. "There are two more trucks up ahead," he said to the farmer. "What will you give me for the whole business?"

"Merryfield Farm," said the farmer. "What else!"

"How big a farm is it?"

"Big enough," said the farmer. "A hundred acres of the best farmland in Crazy County."

"I've always wanted to settle down and have a farm," said Mr. Malone. Then he looked at the farmer. "Can you run a carnival?"

"Reckon so," he said. "Can you run a farm?"

"Don't know," said Mr. Malone, "but I'd like to try." Then he looked at the others. "I'll have to check with my family and friends first."

Terry's mother said, "Oh, yes," and Tim and Wally nodded their heads. Terry wasn't sure what he wanted. He loved the carnival, but then he'd never thought much about farming. He let the others decide.

"It's all right with us," said Wally and Tim. "We're all tired of traveling. But what about the rest of the show?"

"They can manage," said Mr. Malone. "Just as they did before I came along. And maybe Mr. Merryfield can get more work out of them than I could, who knows. It's a deal?"

"Sure," said Mr. Merryfield, and they shook hands all around. And almost before they could blink their eyes, he had made sure they had all their personal belongings

from their truck, clothes and such, and then he got in it and drove off in a hurry to catch up with the two other carnival trucks.

Terry and his family and Wally and Tim climbed into the farmer's truck and drove off in the direction he had pointed to look for Merryfield Farm.

When they found it, it was a fine, wide-open space, with a few buildings and fields that were just bursting with spring.

"Looks good," said Mr. Malone, and he picked up a piece of dirt in his hands and felt it as Terry had seen other farmers do.

"What shall we grow?" Terry asked.

"I don't know," said his father, and he looked in the back of the truck. "There's a lot of stuff in here, but no seeds."

There were no seeds in any of the buildings either, and Wally said, "Guess we'll have to buy some."

"Why," said Terry, "don't we grow something different? Everybody grows things like corn and spinach and turnips, but lots of people don't like vegetables. Why don't we grow something that everybody likes which will make them feel happy?"

"All right," said his father. "What?"

23

"Balloons," said Terry, and he brought from behind his back a small bag of balloons he had taken from the old truck.

"Balloons!" the men all laughed. "You can't grow balloons!"

"Why not?" asked Terry. "From what I hear, anything will grow in Texas."

The men laughed again, but Terry's mother said, "Don't laugh at him. I think he's right." Then she added in a funny voice, "I think he *can* grow balloons."

"Of course I can," said Terry firmly. "Big red ones and blue ones and yellow ones and green ones."

Nobody could think of a good reason not to try it, so they all pitched in and plowed a plot of land and put some fertilizer on it and Terry planted it with bits of balloons from the bag.

While they waited for the balloons to grow, Wally and Tim were busy too. Wally agreed with Terry that farmers grew all the wrong things. "What I'm going to grow," he said, "is something that people never have enough of."

"What's that?" asked Terry.

"Kite string," said Wally. And Terry had to agree that people never did have enough and it was terrible to run out of string just as your kite was so far up in the sky you could hardly see it.

25

So a second plot of land was plowed and Wally seeded it with bits of kite string he just happened to have in his pocket.

Then they all stood back and waited for the wonderful Texas weather to make the kite string grow.

And while they waited, Tim Smoot thought and thought about what to grow on his share of the land. From day to day he changed his mind, and scratched his head, and changed his mind again. At last, when the others were about to give him up, he said, "I'm going to grow baskets."

"Oh, come on," they said. "That's impossible!"

"I don't see why," said Tim. "If Terry can grow balloons, and Wally can grow kite string, why can't I grow baskets? Besides, I just remembered some basket seed a snake charmer with Barnum and Bailey's Circus gave me. I have it in my money box. Besides, I like baskets."

So Tim planted basket seed in the third plowed field, and they all stood back and waited for the wonderful Texas weather to make things grow. The Texas sun shone on the land in the daytime, and the Texas moon shone on it at night. Sometimes the soft Texas rain fell on the land. Something was bound to happen sooner or later.

While they were all waiting, Mrs. Malone cooked for

the men and Terry, and between meals they would lean
against the fence and chew on straws while they talked
about the state of the world. Terry would lean and chew
too, hoping to learn a little something.

"Everybody wants to have more than everybody else,"
said Mr. Malone.

"Why?" asked Terry, but nobody could think of an
answer.

"Nobody wants to help anybody who is in trouble,"
said Wally.

"Why?" asked Terry, and again he got no answer.

"People fight all the time," said Tim, and that seemed
to cover it, for they nodded their heads and agreed.

"Why doesn't somebody change things?" asked Terry,
but he might as well have been talking to himself.

Then after awhile they stopped leaning and chewing and talking and went to look at their crops, for of course, since anything will grow in Texas, all the fields were sprouting like crazy.

Terry's field was the prettiest, with the balloon bushes growing crisp and green in the hot Texas sunshine. Soon the balloons hung like gay little pears on the branches, and every now and then a breeze would come along and

fill them partly with air. Then Terry could see that there were balloons of every shape and size and every color of the rainbow. There were polka-dot balloons and candy-striped balloons. There were even some checkerboard balloons. They were all a mighty pretty sight.

Wally's field did well, too. The kite string vines grew up and up until he had to put in stakes to hold them.

Then the kite string blossoms came out, all purple and blue. After they fell off, the kite string itself began to grow, up and up, higher and higher, sticking up in the air till the whole field looked like the fur on a cat's back when she is talking to a dog.

Tim had to wait longer than the others to see results, for he had been the last to plant, and everyone knows

that baskets are a slow crop. But when they did appear, they were wonderful. On the basket bushes there were long thin baskets for carrying macaroni, and flat round baskets to hold pancakes. There were teeny-tiny baskets to hold sardines and up-side-down baskets to hold up-side-down cake. There were clothes baskets, and waste baskets, and wood baskets, and flower baskets.

The three men, Terry, and his mother were looking at their strange and wonderful fields one morning when a

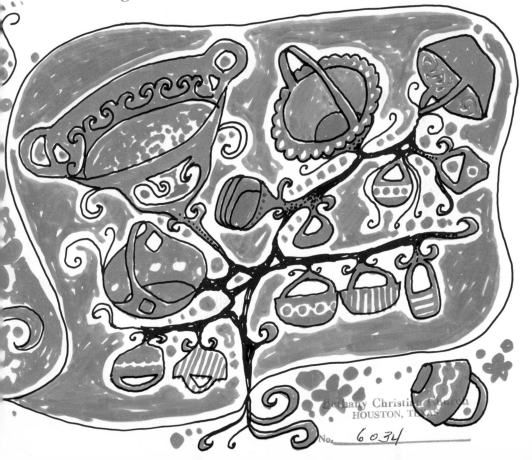

government farm agent drove by. He stopped his car and looked too, with big round eyes.

"Good heavens!" he cried, getting out of the car. "You've started a whole new idea in farming. It may change the world."

"Will it stop people from being selfish?" asked Mr. Malone.

"Will it make people help each other?" asked Wally.

"Will people stop fighting each other?" asked Tim.

"Will it change the world?" asked Terry.

The government man just stood there and looked upset. "I don't know," he said, shaking his head. "I just don't know, but Texas will be proud of you." Then he said, "By the way, if you folks haven't met the candy man down the road, you really should. He has some funny ideas about farming, too."

The next day they drove down to see the candy man.

His name was Mr. Valentine, and he had a crop growing that nearly took their breath away. It was a huge orchard, nearly as big as Rhode Island, and every tree in the orchard grew pink or white or yellow or lavender candy hearts. And every candy heart had a motto on it that said "I Love You" or "Kiss Me Quick" or "You're Great!" or "Say Something Sweet" or "Bee my Honey."

"Pick all you want," said Mr. Valentine. "My problem is not growing them but getting them out to people. I want to give everybody one, but how can I? I spent my last dime for sugar syrup for fertilizer."

"That is a problem," everybody agreed, and they sat down on Mr. Valentine's front porch to think it over.

"People need love," said Mr. Valentine. "But how can I bring it to them?"

"What you need," said Mrs. Malone after awhile, "is something unbelievable. You need a miracle!" The others agreed, and then after awhile they all went home.

Then, because anything can happen in Crazy County, Texas, a miracle began to get underway. It was a good-sized miracle, too. It came in the shape of a big wind, not a tornado or a hurricane, but just a Texas-size wind that began to blow and couldn't seem to stop.

Terry watched from the farmhouse window. That wind was something to see!

First the wind blew crosswise and picked up every balloon in Terry's field, filled it full of air, pulled it off the bush, and carried it over to Wally's field. Then the wind twisted around a bit so that each balloon had a long piece of kite string carefully wrapped around the end of it to hold the air in.

Then the wind swooped down on Tim's field so that the other ends of the pieces of kite string were fastened around the handles of Tim's baskets.

The gay balloons with the baskets hanging from them then blew with the wind down the road to Mr. Valentine's farm, where the wind danced them around the trees until each basket was filled to the brim with candy hearts with mottoes on them.

Then the wind stopped blowing sidewise and began to blow up, and all the baskets and balloons went high, high up into the blue sky. They went up so high that two astronauts on their way to the moon saw them and couldn't believe their eyes.

Then the Texas wind blew north, south, east, and west like anything and all at the same time, and the baskets blew miles and miles away. Then the wind blew downward, and the baskets began to float to earth in Oregon and Alabama and Illinois and Arizona and Vermont. Baskets fell on Seattle and Denver and Detroit and Baltimore and Memphis.

They fell on farms and factories, on shops and schools, on theaters and baseball fields and railroad stations and swimming pools and airports.

And they fell on people—all kinds of people. In Boston two old men with white hair sat on either end of a park bench on Boston Common. They were in business, each trying to make more money than the other, and they hadn't spoken to each other in twenty years. A basket full of candy hearts landed on the bench between them.

The first old man reached in and took out a candy heart—a red one. "Bee My Honey" it said, and he laughed out loud. The second old man took a pink heart from the basket, and it said "Say Something Sweet," and then he laughed. And then they both laughed, and talked to each other about their grandchildren and forgot about money and became good friends.

In New York City two big taxi drivers had just bumped into each other on a busy street. They had jumped from their taxis ready to fight when a basket landed on the sidewalk.

"Kiss Me" said a yellow heart when the first driver read it. "Say Something Sweet" read the heart the second driver took from the basket. They looked at each other in surprise.

"Well, well," they said. "Things aren't so bad, are they?" and they grinned at each other, shook hands, and went off to have a cup of coffee together.

Far out in Kansas a big yellow school bus crossed the flat prairies like a great caterpillar. The bus driver was tired and the children were noisy and full of tricks.

"Quiet!" yelled the driver. "Quiet, or I'll stop the bus." But they were not quiet, and he stopped the bus and made them all get out, and as they stood in the dusty road beside the bus a basket of candy hearts floated down to them.

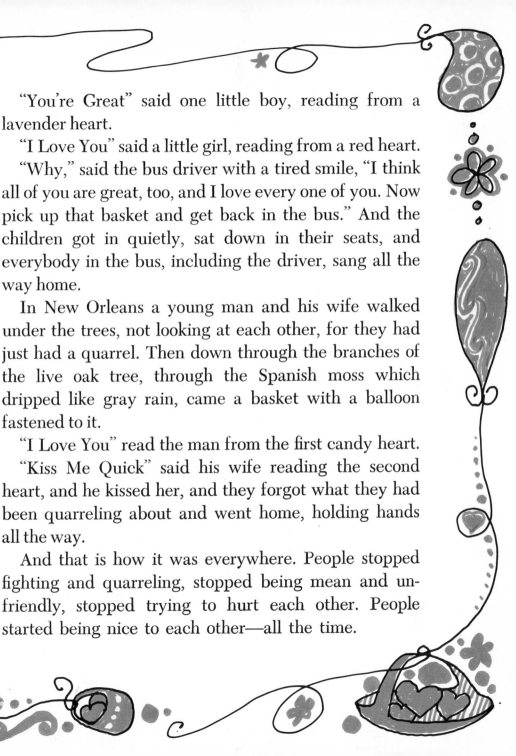

"You're Great" said one little boy, reading from a lavender heart.

"I Love You" said a little girl, reading from a red heart.

"Why," said the bus driver with a tired smile, "I think all of you are great, too, and I love every one of you. Now pick up that basket and get back in the bus." And the children got in quietly, sat down in their seats, and everybody in the bus, including the driver, sang all the way home.

In New Orleans a young man and his wife walked under the trees, not looking at each other, for they had just had a quarrel. Then down through the branches of the live oak tree, through the Spanish moss which dripped like gray rain, came a basket with a balloon fastened to it.

"I Love You" read the man from the first candy heart.

"Kiss Me Quick" said his wife reading the second heart, and he kissed her, and they forgot what they had been quarreling about and went home, holding hands all the way.

And that is how it was everywhere. People stopped fighting and quarreling, stopped being mean and un-friendly, stopped trying to hurt each other. People started being nice to each other—all the time.

The Malones and Terry? Wally and Tim? And Mr. Valentine? You want to know what happened to them? Well, that great big wind picked them up, too, just as it had picked up the balloons and the kite string and the baskets and the candy hearts. The wind took Terry and his mother and father, Wally, Tim, and Mr. Valentine up, up, up in the air, and it landed them ever so gently on an island, a very small island, in the South Pacific.

Of course, nobody really knows, but we imagine they started farming again, right away, growing balloons—kite strings—baskets—and candy hearts. And we know that wherever they are, they are making people happy.